I0529680

A HINT OF FAERY

MAGICAL SHORT STORIES, VOLUME 1

T. THORN COYLE

PF

ISBN: 978-1-946476-15-9

Things had grown so strange, he honestly didn't know if he could take it anymore. The stack of library books piled on the floor wasn't helping. Neither was his favorite playlist.

All he could do was return to the story inside his head...

A BRIEF INTRODUCTION FROM THE AUTHOR

Magical animals. Bargains. People that are not quite...human. Glimmerings of spaces that exist around the edges of what we call real.

Stories that explore I have loved these sorts of tales for decades. Stories that invoke the magic of faery, and that turn the ordinary world upside down, even if only for a few pages? They're the stories I return to, again and again.

These days, along with reading those tales, I write them.

Here's a collection of five, all written with the support of my amazing Patreon friends. Some of these short tales have appeared in other collections, some not, but nonetheless these five stories all wanted to live together beneath one cover.

So here they are: faery foxes, magic cats,

pookahs, talking rabbit's heads, and the best ice cream in all the worlds.

Crack open the door and enter...

T. Thorn Coyle
   Portland, Oregon
   2020

THE DAY THE MAGIC FOX APPEARED

W hat a shitty day.

It was roasting hot outside. I was sweating, and my bike had gotten a flat tire en route home from work. And before that, I'd had to stop some stupid assholes from harassing the houseless guy that panhandled in front of the game store. People being jerks seemed to be on the rise.

Plus, I was hangry.

Ignoring my growling stomach, I pushed my way into the bathroom down the hall. The house felt empty. Housemates were all still at work. That was good. I could use a little quiet.

I splashed cold water on my face in the cracked white basin, and reached, for the bright orange towel.

It moved. I swore it did.

Don't be a doofus, Candy.

I grabbed the towel and mopped at my face then spluttered.

My lips were stuck with... fur?

"Gross! What the hell?"

I blinked, and scraped my hands across my face, trying to clear the disgusting whatever-it-was from my mouth and cheeks. Fur, like hair, sticks to wet things. I needed a towel. My towel.

"Sorry about that," said a small, raspy voice.

"Poor timing on my part. But I really needed to talk to you."

My heart pounded and sweat broke out on the back of my neck. Whipping my head around, I scanned the room one-eyed, the other eye shut against what was likely one thin strand of fur but felt like a whole sweater.

I looked down, and leapt back, crashing into the shower door. "Ouch!"

There was a fox in the bathroom. A big fox. All orange and bristly, with black paws, a black nose, and a damn white tip on its bushy tail.

"What the hell?"

"You're repeating yourself, so I will, too. I apologize for my poor timing." The fox started speaking slowly, as if to a small child whom it really needed to understand. Its black tipped snout moved, though I had no idea how it was forming human words. "I... need... to... speak... with..."

"Oh, cut it out! I hear you. Just... go to the kitchen! I've got to wash my face again. If you've left me any clean towels!"

"Oh, that towel is quite clean, I assure you. Or as clean as it was when I arrived. You may wish to change it out though. It smells as if you've been using it for at least a week, and towels are bacteria breeding grounds..."

I pointed to the door. "Out."

The fox dipped its head, then trotted past me on dainty black feet. I shoved the door closed and looked down at the towel. No fur. I sniffed it. The fox was right. The towel needed changing. But I could deal with that later.

Hanging the towel back on the rack, I turned the water back on and bent to wash my face. I used soap this time.

I opened the bathroom door and heard the soft rumble of the electric kettle and the clink of spoons. What the hell? Yeah. Maybe I needed a different phrase. But this whole situation was utterly surreal. Sure, a fox cleric was my go-to RPG character, but that didn't mean I expected an actual talking fox to have shown up and done something weird to my towel.

Or be able to work my kettle.

As I clopped my sneaker'd feet down the bright hallway, I tried to get my shit together. I entered the red and white decorated kitchen with the worn black and white linoleum tiles, and the clacking Felix-the-Cat wall clock. The fox had dragged a chair over to the crappy white countertop and was pulling a mug from the cupboard with its mouth. I about lost it.

"How the?" Great, Candy. Real articulate.

But really? All I had wanted was to get my limping bicycle home, wash my face, and stare out the living room with a cup of tea in hand. I was so not prepared for a face full of fur and a fox in my kitchen.

"You're pretty easily surprised for a person who spends so much time dreaming up ogres and wizards and going on whole adventures with them. Do you take milk in your tea?"

The fox looked at me with big dark eyes rimmed in white and black. For the first time I noticed, it was kind of beautiful.

Saying nothing, I walked to the 'fridge and pulled out a small carton of half-and-half.

"How are you gonna pour that?" I finally asked, jerking my chin toward the shiny red electric kettle.

"By using your hands," it replied, cool and calm as you please.

I set the carton down, got two tea bags from the glass canister on the countertop, and poured. The fox trotted over to the small red table tucked by the window that looked out onto our overgrown back-yard. Hopping up on one of the white wooden chairs, tail curled around its black paws, the fox sat straight-backed. Waiting for me.

"Do you take milk in your tea?" I asked. Two could play the cool-as-you-please game.

The fox tilted its long snout down. "Of course," it replied.

Of course a magic talking faery fox takes milk in its tea, I thought. What else would you expect?

I plunked the heavy mugs down on the table and sat down. Scrubbing my hands across my face, I released a sigh.

You'd think I would feel ecstatic to have a talking fox in my kitchen, but really? Sometimes a person just wants an ordinary life, you know? No matter how much we play at knights and castles, dragons and magic amulets, we actually just want a stable job that pays the bills and a place to sleep at night.

The fox sniffed at the steam curling out of the mug.

"So," I picked up my mug and took a sip. "What's your name? And are you going to explain what you're doing here? Also, my towel? Seriously? What kind of magical creature uses a towel as a portal, for Gods' sakes?"

The fox lapped at the tea, long tongue flicking out delicately, rolling the liquid into its mouth.

"My name is Tracy," it said. "And why not a towel?"

"I thought you..." I waved a hand in the air, "types."

The fox arched one bushy eyebrow.

"You know, faeries, magical beings, whatever," I continued. "I thought you used mirrors as portals."

The fox sighed and lapped up more tea. I was amazed that it could drink from a mug and not spill anything. I could barely manage that some days.

"Different beings use different things. I like towels. They're soft and easy to manage. Mirrors are hard and cold and feel weird when you're halfway through. Walking through a towel is like walking through a sunbeam. Besides, what makes you so sure I'm a magical being?"

I shook my head.

"That towel thing is bizarre, but okay. And why do I think you're magic? Come on. You use towels as inter-dimensional portals, and you talk. Plus..." I paused and gave the animal another look. "You kind of glow around the edges."

The fox didn't reply. I took that as a yes, I'm magical but not admitting it, answer.

"Not being a magical fox myself," I said, "I'll take your word for the portal thing. And I hope you give me some credit here for not being a gibbering mess on the floor right now. Most people would be, you know."

I could swear the fox smiled.

"That's why I'm here," it said. "You're not most people."

Now, everyone wants to hear they're special, but color me skeptical. Telling someone "you're not like other fill-in-the-group" is the oldest con in the book.

It was my turn to raise an eyebrow. So I did, and drank more tea. A hummingbird buzzed the window. The fox jerked its head toward the glass and gave that snout-dipping nod again. The hummer buzzed away.

Okay. Were all the local creatures in on this?

"What I mean," the fox continued, "is that you have a unique confluence of an open and curious mind, a flexible sense of reality, no family you're responsible for, and you already have skills in the area I'm interested in pursuing."

"And what area is that?"

"You understand fantasy role-playing games."

"You want us to what?" Rina yelped. We were hanging out in the living room, arrayed on the cozy overstuffed couch, feet up on the battered coffee table. Rina, a short, curvy, brown-skinned creampuff of badass, tapped the toes of her boots together in irritation.

"Yeah," said Solomon, lighting up a joint. "I don't get this at all."

A big, pasty, Jewish dude with five o'clock shadow and a black leather kippah, he sat on one of the matching club chairs covered in fake-tapestry-blankets with stylized dragons on them. What can I say? We're geeks, and we're relatively broke. He passed the joint my way. I handed it to Rina.

Things were weird enough as it was. I needed as clear a head as possible to explain the entity hiding out in my bedroom.

Tracy.

A talking fox.

"I'll need you to suspend disbelief for a minute. Pretend you're in a new RPG, okay?"

Rina huffed and crossed her arms over her ample chest. Solomon took another puff on the joint and nodded before tapping it out in an ashtray. He was a two puff a day guy.

"A magic fox came to us with a proposition."

"To us?" Rina asked. Maybe she needed more pot. That one puff hadn't made her any more chill, that's for sure.

"Yes. Well, to me, first. But it can use our help."

"And what is it that this fox wants us to do?" Solomon asked.

"It needs humans to collaborate on a game. To seed more magic in the world, it said." I was kind of wishing I'd taken a hit off the joint now. Rubbing my hands on my jeans, I took a breath. "It says the realm of faery is in danger of completely separating from the human world if more humans don't start to believe."

Solomon leaned forward, elbows on the knees of his black cargo pants. "Seems like that would be a good thing for faery," he said. "Less interference by human bullshit. Just let us go our way. Make our own mistakes. Orchestrate our own demise."

"Well, that's cheerful," Rina said. She touched my arm. "I still don't get it, though, Candy. Are you making shit up? Or is this fox real? Like physically real? Or what?"

I angled my head and called up the stairs.

"Tracy! We're ready for you!"

Well, that was an overstatement, wasn't it? No one could be ready for a talking fox.

Tracy's slender orange form appeared at the top of the oak staircase.

"You called me?" Their raspy voice was quiet, barely audible over Solomon's heavy breathing and the strange, mewling noise Rina was making with her throat.

"Yes. It seemed simpler to introduce you in person. Come down?"

Tracy barely made a sound on the creaky old stairs, disappearing behind the couch for a moment, before emerging into the living room.

"Holy shit," Solomon breathed out. "You're an actual, talking fox. Just like in the games."

Tracy leapt up onto the other chair, circling three times before settling onto the second dragon fake-tapestry-blanket.

"What do you want to know?" the fox asked.

Rina and Solomon looked at each other. Then at me.

They both avoided looking at the fox.

"Go ahead," I finally said. "What do you want to ask?"

Rina swallowed, hard. She was trembling a little. I stopped myself from reaching out to grab her hand. I had a feeling this was something she had to do herself.

"So..." her voice was reedy, as if she wasn't getting enough air. Rina cleared her throat and tried again. "Candy says you need help. That faery will separate from the world or something?"

"That's right," Tracy replied.

"And why isn't that a good thing?" Solomon asked, running a hand over his stubble.

The fox fixed him with its dark gaze. Solomon stared right back. I was impressed. He seemed to be recovering quickly, though I could see his fingers tapping, likely wanting to light up the joint again.

"If the realms separate completely, one of the worlds will die."

The words hung in the air like smoke from a California wildfire.

"And it won't be faery, will it?" Rina asked.

Tracy gave a little shrug of its small, umber shoulders. "Could go either way. But the way humans are going so far? It's likely that your realm will be the one to die. Or at least your race."

"Like, the human race?" Solomon rumbled.

"Exactly," Tracy replied.

Solomon and Rina both looked at me again, waiting for me to say something. To be the Dungeon Master in charge of this new game.

"If you're in," I said, "we should order up a pizza and make a plan."

Solomon slipped his cell from one of the many pockets on his cargo pants and hit dial. He had at least three pizza places programmed into his phone.

"One meat, one veggie okay?"

"Extra cheese, please," the fox said.

"You eat pizza?" I asked.

"Doesn't everyone?" it replied.

That was five years ago.

Slowly, the story came out. Tracy had been

watching me for a while, peering through curtain fabric and towels, making sure I was the right one. I didn't want to think about that too hard. If Tracy saw some things that were embarrassing, the fox kept it to itself.

I now have a pretty good job running a small gaming company, with Rina and Solomon as my seconds in command. Together, we've made enough to put a down payment on a house. Who wants to live alone? Our friends test drive the games, for the price of a pizza and snacks.

Tracy literally pops in once a week to confer.

What does Tracy get out of it? The fox insists we're saving the world. Sometimes I still find that hard to believe.

But then again, we're still here, aren't we?

And anything that makes the world a little more fun and magical? That's okay by me.

2

THE RABBIT'S HEAD

The heavy, five paneled oak bedroom door shut behind me with a thunk. There was no reason to shut it at all, seeing as I was the only one living in the apartment carved out of the hundred- and fifty-year-old building, but childhood habits stick. At least, they do with me.

Though I'd grown up with the full run of the entire manse and it's generous backyard, I'd gotten used to living in the smaller space. I liked it, actually. The apartments that had so scandalized my family members when the project was first proposed suited me just fine. The renovations had made the space friendlier and more cozy.

Hurrying down the well worn red and blue Persian runner, I slung my black backpack over my shoulders and reached up to adjust my lavender tie. I was almost to the front door when I was stopped short by the damn sense that someone was looking at me.

I cursed under my breath, dropped my hands, and looked up.

There it was, fur gleaming white in the sunshine.

The rabbit's head looked down and stared. Judging. Its creepy red glass eyes refracted the light pouring through the diamond-paned windows set into white walls above the dark wainscoting that defined the long hallway.

The Hall to Nowhere we called it when bored on long, rainy days.

Nowhere, except, once again, here I was, trying to leave. Being judged by a taxidermied rabbit's head.

It always judged. And there was never any way to measure up. The rabbit's head had judged my first attempts to crawl. It had judged my acne scored cheeks. It had judged my tears when Father died.

Fucker.

"Your tie is crooked."

My hand jerked toward my neck, reflexively, before I willed it back down again. I would not adjust my tie, crooked or not. I wouldn't. It was a matter of principle to not do what the rabbit's head said. The damn thing was so bossy and had been since I first noticed it staring down at me

"Made you check," it said. So petty. So snide. So. Damn. Superior.

"Piss off," I replied, keeping my voice steady and calm. It wouldn't do to let the head know it rattled me.

I'd tried to get rid of it over the years. It was trotted out of boxes at a few rummage sales, but was carted right back home again. I tried to donate it to a charity shop, who thanked me promptly but said they had no room for taxidermy.

The rubbish bin wouldn't take it, either. Wouldn't even open up its lid.

The damn rabbit's head had everyone, and every thing, entranced by its strange magic. We were all under its fucking spell.

All because great grandfather wanted to impress his lady love with the damned rabbit's foot she wanted. "*For luck,*" she had said. So he had to kill the damn thing, dress the right foot, and make a cunning little, metal cap for the top of the bloody stump.

And then, the twisted carcass spoke.

"*You have stolen my happy life and must bear the curse.*"

Grandfather dropped his knife, the story says, and pierced his right big toe. He walked with a slight limp from that day forward. He also, legend has it, once he got his bleeding under control, chopped the head from the carcass to get the thing to shut up.

That only made it worse.

"What do you want?" I asked, feeling peevish. I was running late again, this time to the first job interview I'd had in months that I was actually looking forward to. I didn't want just any job. It didn't need to be heroic, but I wanted to do something at least marginally meaningful.

"Tsk tsk," the rabbit said, tongue rasping against its long front teeth. "Is that any way to talk to a magical rabbit's head?"

By force of will, I did not roll my eyes, but stood in what I hoped looked like a respectful posture.

"Well?" the head would not let the insult slide.

I sighed and dragged the toes of my shoes across the backs of my slacks. I hadn't had time to polish them this week. May as well give them a quick buff while I was standing here.

"My apologies, oh rabbit's head. Is there something you require of me?"

The small pink nose sniffed, which was odd if you thought about it. It sounded like a human nose, sniffing.

Of course, the rabbit was also talking, so...

I dragged my thoughts back to the white whiskers that quivered two feet above my head.

"I require," it said, "to receive my due. To take up my former occupation. To..."

"You know this isn't possible. We've discussed it ad nauseam." Literally. I was thoroughly sick of the rabbit's head, the discussion, and the damned mess it had made of my life.

"I have to go. I'm late."

"For a very important date?"

I swore the thing sneered, though varied facial expressions weren't its strong points.

"Clever," I replied. "For a job interview."

"Whatever do you need money for?" The red glass eyes swiveled in their sockets. "You have this lovely place to lay your head, and me for company."

"I need food. And WiFi. And a phone. And my

bicycle needs servicing, and..." I stopped. Damn it. I was justifying myself to the damn white rabbit once again. "How do you do that?"

"Do what?" Cool as a cucumber, the head was. If it still had nails, it would buff them. I hated the rabbit, but I wouldn't give it the satisfaction of whining. Not today.

"Nothing."

I turned, yanked open the apartment door, and fled down the wide oak stairs to the main entrance, hoping against hope I hadn't missed my bus.

The boy irritated the rabbit. He was so... weak. Now, the boy's grandfather had been a proper adversary. Someone the rabbit could sink his teeth into, so to speak. As a matter of fact, when the old man had grabbed the rabbit it had, indeed, sunk its front teeth into the webbing of his right hand and tore through the flesh. All these years later, he could still taste the sweetness of his blood.

This boy, though...something must be done. The rabbit would be stuck in this poky hallway, all alone, with no children to admire the fine tilt of his head, or tell one another stories about how powerful and frightening he was. He missed all of that, mightily.

But the boy was cowed, and children were highly

unlikely. He never even had friends around. Life itself had failed him and the boy expected nothing less.

"What he needs is a proper spine... But I suppose he may need a little luck to begin with. Damn it."

The rabbit hated the thought, but nonetheless, just as the rabbit took luck away, so the rabbit could grant it once again.

"Why do you want to work with us?"

The woman wore jeans, and a long-sleeved T-shirt. I had totally overdressedm but she looked at me as if that didn't matter a whit. A half smile graced her well scrubbed, milk pale face, as if she expected something wonderful in reply.

Extroverts. They *always* seem to expect something wonderful to emerge from human interactions.

You're projecting. I heard my former therapist's voice inside my head. My one true friend, I'd let him go when the money started running out.

"Mr. Green?"

"Sorry. To be honest, I need a job."

One pale eyebrow raised. "I believe that much is clear."

"And..." I swallowed, "my mother loved plants, and, with my IT skills, helping a large nursery like yourselves set up web systems seemed like a way to keep her memory alive."

I looked out the window at people bustling by, then back at her, then realized what I'd said was true.

"Maybe I'll take up gardening again. I haven't since..."

She nodded, as if she understood, not prompting me to finished the sentence that still dangled in the air between us. I couldn't very well tell her that my mother wasn't dead, just wasn't *here*. She'd bunked off to South America with the gardener after Father died and all the trouble started. I hadn't seen her in years.

Mother had said she wanted "a fresh start. I can't bear to see the house chopped up. And I cannot bear that rabbit anymore."

But it was fine for me to stay, wasn't it? Fine for me to live in a construction zone for months, and drink tea while dodging falling plaster. It was fine to stick *me* with Grandfather's damned rabbit's head.

"I have loads of computer experiences, and loads of experience with plants, even though it's been a while. If you'll just give me a chance..."

The sympathy on her face warred with slight distaste.

Cardinal job hunting rule number one: Never seem too desperate. Well, then. Blew that.

"We'll call you," she said, then rose and stuck out a hand. "Thank you for coming in, Mr. Green."

Her handshake was firm. Dry. I did my best to match it, before picking up my backpack and shuffling toward the door. At least I made certain my back was straight.

Luck was a small magic, part of the larger magics of rabbits everywhere. The magics they had learned to hide once the humans started hunting them, not for the meat of their flesh, or the warmth of their fur—which rabbits abhorred and feared, but at least things that an animal could understand—but for their feet. Which was ridiculous. The feet of a rabbit held no more magic than any other part. But humans were a superstitious lot, and latched onto the smallest fancies, insisting they were true.

Thankfully, the "lucky" rabbit's feet trend had fallen out of fashion, which was one good thing about human fancies. So at least Humbert did not have to worry as much as he used to about the other rabbit clans.

He'd been a priest of several clans, once upon a time, which is where he got his extra strength. It was the only reason his consciousness had not fled his body immediately upon death. He had compelled the grandfather to not throw his head on the compost heap, where his being would have dissolved along with his flesh.

As long as the head of the priest was preserved, intelligence survived.

And it was time, long past time, he realized, that he used that intelligence again, and turn this boy's life around.

Because the boy certainly would not do it on his own. And without that change, the rabbit was condemned to boredom for as long as the boy lived, and perhaps even beyond.

The bus rumbled and hissed and smelled of fried potatoes and Bay Rum cologne. Not my favorite combination, though the potatoes made me hungry.

My name is Felix. Ironic, I know. Father and Mother had hoped the name would ameliorate the cursed influence of Grandfather's rabbit's head.

It didn't. As a boy and teen, I was gangly, awkward, withdrawn, and stumbling. None of these qualities were the classics that set a person up for success in life. Unfortunately, I hadn't outgrown them.

Sighing, I pulled the bell cord and shoved my way through backpacks and solid shoulders. Reaching the back exit, I pushed hard against the doors. As the soles of my leather shoes touched down on the sidewalk, I saw her, cloud of dark hair floating above plump, rounded shoulders. Brows furrowed beneath green framed glasses as she stared down at her phone. I couldn't quite see her eyes, but I just knew that they were beautiful.

Her bright red dress was covered in a pattern of a white rabbit in heraldic dress, holding a golden trumpet in one paw. Alice.

I stumbled, tripped, and fell, backpack smacking the back of my head as my knees cracked against the concrete.

"Oh my God! Are you okay?"

Her voice was like sunshine breaking through clouds.

And then she crouched next to me, smelling of honeysuckle and warm skin. And I was right. Here eyes were as beautiful as the rest of her. Bright with intelligence. A rich, chocolate brown.

I felt a flush stain my cheeks. Damn it.

"I... I... I'm fine!" I blurted and struggled to rise. She reached out to help me. As her hand touched mine, I hissed with pain. She dropped it.

"You're hurt!"

"Just scraped." I pushed myself up off my

bruised knees, swaying a bit as my backpack thunked back down into place. My right hand hurt like anything.

"Can I help you somewhere?"

I shook my head. "Thanks, but, I'm almost home." Where I would have to climb stairs. My knees ached just thinking about it.

"If you're sure…" she seemed dubious.

He had used just a bit of magic. A sprinkling of possibility winging the boy's way.

If the dolt required more, the rabbit would supply it. But he trusted neither his magics, lain dormant for so many years, nor the boy himself. What if he overloaded the fumbling ass, and he became ill, or worse, died? And then, what if the rabbit ended up in the dreaded rummage sale for good this time?

Hanging there on the wall, watching the sunlight shift across the dusty walls, awaiting the boy's return, the rabbit's nose twitched in horror.

No. He had used just the right amount of magic. The boy would be fine, and his luck would change, that very day, in fact.

Unless the boy was further gone than the rabbit realized.

Magic needed an opening, no matter how small, in order to be applied.

But surely the boy was still malleable enough? Not so old and set in his ways...

"Is there a good place to eat around here?"

I found it hard to parse the words coming out of her mouth. I'd been ready to shuffle off in shame, but here she was, gazing earnestly at my face, asking me about food. Was she asking me to lunch?

I cleared my throat. "Uh. Yeah. There's a place around the corner. Salad, sandwiches, you know. Basic stuff. But it's really good."

I pointed to the intersection behind us, showing her where it was. Hope that she was asking me to lunch warred alongside hope that she would go on her way and leave me to nurse my wounds in peace.

Honestly? I didn't know which outcome I preferred.

"Are you hungry?" she asked.

My heart lifted. I guess I did know. I had made a decision. Damn the rabbit's curse, I wanted this.

"Yes. I am. May I join you?"

She smiled and gave a slight nod.

I couldn't help but smile back.

If all went well, the boy would grow less *boring*, at least. Human children took a long time to be interesting, and who knew if the bit of luck the rabbit had thrown the boy's way would be enough to hook another human long enough to bear a squalling babe, let alone allow the child to grow enough to become interesting.

But in the old days, the house was large, and filled with other people, not just the dreary boy. The rabbit had heard shouts of laughter and whispered conversations. New people would always pause, and admire him. For a time, he had held pride of place in a more central location, where people gathered, and drank strange, caustic liquids that made them dance.

And they paid attention to him. The boy was so dull and stupid, the only way the rabbit could get any attention at all was through needling the creature. And he wearied of it.

Oh! How he longed for the days when rabbits traveled for miles to seek his counsel. He had not dreamed about those times for decades, but lately, the dreams had returned, filling his mouth with the taste of dandelion and green grass. He awakened, nose twitching and eyes wet with weeping.

Those days would never come, but at least he could make life more interesting again.

He just wanted one being to look upon him with admiration instead of disgust. If that had to be a human? He would settle.

For the rabbit was no fool. A wise rabbit took what he could get.

Her name was Rhonda. She was looking for a place to live, just arrived from a city far away. She laughed at his jokes.

Her favorite comic book was Saga.

I could not believe my luck.

While she was away, washing her hands, I watched the people on the sidewalk outside, everyone heading somewhere. I had washed mine immediately. The right one still stung, but at least it wasn't filthy. And though my knees felt like hell, I hadn't torn my best trousers, which felt like a minor miracle.

I finally noticed my fingers tapped idly on the phone. I'd just check my email quickly, before she came back. My breath quickened...and then my jaw dropped.

"Did something happen?" She was back.

"I, uh...no. Yeah. I mean..." I looked up at her, still standing there, expectant look on her face. *Don't blow this, asshole.* Cardinal rule of dating—so I'd heard—

don't check email when a gorgeous woman is staring at you. But...

"Can you give me a sec?" I had to read the thing. "I think the job interview I had this morning just emailed me."

"Sure." She slid into the bench across the table, the white rabbits on her dress rippling across her chest as she scooted herself in. Damn.

I lowered my eyes back to my email. "Thanks."

Scanning the scant paragraph of text, my jaw dropped yet again.

"Good news?"

Things like this never happened to me. Never.

"It seems too soon for this, but..." I glanced down, and then back up again. Her brown eyes held steady. "They want me to come back in for a second round. They actually liked me!"

Her brow furrowed. "And why wouldn't they?"

No way was I answering that, so I just shrugged, put down the phone, and smiled. All of a sudden, smiling felt easy.

"Ready to order?"

He heard footsteps. They sounded different. Lighter. Then the scrape of key in lock. The dark wood door opened. The light changed.

And there stood the boy, barely recognizable as the creature who had left scant hours before.

He had a smile on his face. As a matter of fact, he was grinning ear to ear.

The boy slung the pack from his shoulders and dropped it to the floor.

"You'll never guess what happened to me today!" There was excitement in the boy's voice. Interest. Life. And he was talking to the rabbit without prompting.

"What, pray-tell, happened to you today?"

"I think I may have gotten a job. And a girlfriend. Or... well... a friend at least. We'll see. But, yeah...I had a good day. A really, really, good day."

He picked up the pack from the floor and sauntered—sauntered!—down the hallway toward his room

The rabbit gave a sigh of relief. The burst of magic had been enough. Enough to set the wheels in motion. Enough to make a change. He had not lost his magic. But perhaps another nudge...

"You will bring this friend over? Introduce us?"

The boy paused. Turned. Stared up at the rabbit. "Sure. Why not?"

Those were the words the rabbit had been waiting for, all of these years, though he had never realized it until now. The boy had not asked a curious question for so long.

"Hey," the boy asked. "Why are you being nice to me, anyway?"

"Perhaps I just wanted a change."

Waking up in my high bed the next morning, I could barely believe my luck. Sure, my knees hurt, but I had a second job interview, and plans to see Rhonda again.

And the rabbit wasn't being an asshole anymore.

Maybe my life was turning itself around.

I was determined to help it along.

3

I NEVER CAUGHT HER NAME

. . .

My fingers clutched at the collar of my black wool coat, pulling it tighter in defense against the wind coming across the river.

The Liffey is no grand thing, no wide rush of water like the Boyne, but it is beautiful all the same. Crossed by footbridges and larger auto bridges that join the north of the city to the south, and the business district of Dublin with the frenetic tourist's heart of Temple Bar, the Liffey runs on, sometimes sparkling and sometimes a bit murky with the muck of low tide.

That evening, the river smelled slightly of green algae and old mud churned up from the bottom as the tide slowly rose again to greet the walkers, pram pushers, and bench dozers. The river smells mixed in the dimming light with the scent of combusting tobacco, and the wash of Italian aftershave.

Two brown gulls were in a standoff over a discarded sandwich on the walkway, and a flock of crows called out overhead. The gloaming slowly washed out the streets, sun fading in flashes on blue tiles and gray stone.

A glimmer of color sparked by the freshly turned on street lamps caught my attention. Glancing to my left, I found myself staring at the image of a dragon bent on destroying the city painted on roll up doors of shops not too long closed. The dragon snaked from shop door to shop door, rampaging as it went.

A man bumped up against me, not expecting my sudden stop on the walkway. My leather bag with its shiny butch snaps slammed against my hip in his wake.

"Sorry mate," I called after him. The slapping of his leather-soled shoes on the walkway was the only response.

It was an evening for wandering and my thick boot heels measured out the city with their own rhythm. The rhythm of the dispossessed.

That night–the night I met her for the first time–I was a woman with no home. No one to get back to. No lover waiting over a pint in a cozy snug of a bar. Six months I'd been this way. Not quite looking, but somehow expecting someone to turn a corner, a smile of recognition lighting up their face as they quickened their pace toward me.

That never happened. Never. Even when I was with someone. Guess I wasn't the face-lighting-up type. I settled for good sex and better conversation.

I didn't mind it much. I enjoyed wandering alone. Except for when I didn't. Walking the river helped my research as much as poring over the crumbling books that lined my study. It was walk, or drink too many pints. And I couldn't smoke in pubs anymore, making sitting in them alone all the less enticing. Fuckin' health Puritans.

My clever fingers–named as such by a satisfied lover one night–drew a cardboard packet of ciggies out from one of my coat pockets. Tapping out a pale cylinder out, I slipped it between my lips. The wheel of my lighter snicked into a spark.

Oh yes. Yes. Yes. Yes. Burning paper and tobacco. Just as delicious as the first time I'd ever put one in my mouth, going on twenty years now.

I was fifteen then, and Harry and I had met behind the library. I don't know what took more courage from me that day, the first kiss or the first cigarette. The kiss was a bit too wet for my taste, leaving my chin sopping with spit. The cigarette though, that was clean and dry. And it made me feel dangerous. I liked that.

"Huh." I laughed at myself. I still loved my cigs, but what I wouldn't give for a kiss these days. A pressing of lips against my own. A little warmth. A little moistness. One small sigh. An opening into another's heart. Just like that. Simple. Man or woman, didn't matter.

My last partner had been Patricia. She who had named my fingers "clever," and wheeled alongside me on my rambles, chair wheels shushing in and out of puddles on the ubiquitous rainy Dublin days. She hated my smoking. The sex was great, but... she wanted a more steady life than I could ever offer.

"You're too self-absorbed, Max." I couldn't help but agree. At least, I could see why it seemed that way. But really, it wasn't that I was self-obsessed, I was obsessed with magic. It took over everything else. Preoccupied me, not leaving much space for occupation by anything or anyone else.

I obsessed over Yeat's crazy painted cards and tools. Obsessed over Faerie stories and windswept mounds. Obsessed myself with listening in tumbling stone cairns for the voices of the long since dead.

Obsessed with tracing magic through piles of books, not quite discovering whether or not magic itself was true, or whether everyone who dipped their toes into that river were just crazy.

"Mad, dead, or a poet," described much of Ireland. The joke was that most of my library were books collected or written by folks who were all three.

My research grant was a pittance and the tutoring I did barely paid for my rent, but I just couldn't seem to stop. Up past midnight and awake again at six, fingers dry from turning paper and ink-stained turquoise from my fountain pen.

So now, Patricia six months gone and no one yet to replace her, the crack of my boots on cobblestones and the taste of tobacco were my only constant companions. The love affairs that wouldn't quit.

White painted wrought iron curved just ahead of me. The Ha'Penny Bridge. A bit of white-painted Victorian frippery spanning the river. Curlicues arched across the narrow, iron footbridge, rising to v'd peaks in the center. Misshapen lumps glommed onto the risers, marring the graceful turns and curves.

They were constellations of locks without keys. Bits of folk magic. Wishes dangling in the coming night.

This far away, I couldn't distinguish the lumps as locks, but I knew that they were there. Tourists crossed this bridge, drunk on holiday and too many pints in Temple Bar, leaving little bits of their hopes and dreams upon the bridge. Little did they know how lucky they were to have escaped the streets unscathed. Some of them likely hadn't.

Hearts locked and pockets picked, all in one go.

Pick-pocketing is a fine art here. I discovered that the hard way after moving to the city, barely keeping my wallet after an apprentice tried to nick it from my back pocket. I kept nothing in my back pockets after that. Nothing but a handkerchief, and they were welcome to those. I still lost one occasionally, and considered it a white linen offering to the Gods of the Streets.

Speaking of which, it was getting on time to make another offering soon. Offerings kept the streets friendly to my footsteps at all hours of day or night. A person alone needed all the help she could get.

"Rank superstition" Patricia would have said. I tell you, if it hadn't been for the strong and easy sex, and her gorgeous eyes and arms, I wouldn't have stayed with her as long as I did. Nor she, with me. The only ways we fit together were in a love for old films and the way our bodies moved together in bed.

She was a scientist. Worked for one of the big pharma places outside the city. Spinning proteins out of cells. Measuring. Testing. Wheeling around the shiny chrome and white in her lab coat. Anything that didn't require a sterile clean room, that's the work she did.

I broached the steps of the bridge. It was my favorite, with its fanciful white curves. And I loved the locks, even though–according to all the research and fumbling experimentation I had done–they were bad magic. I just loved that ordinary people still believed enough in magic to make a go of it. To seal their troth to one another's hearts and throw the key away into the waters down below, leaving a metal lock on this Dublin bridge forever.

Or until a city worker came to cut it down.

That night, a woman sat there, on the bridge. Hat

tucked down over her ears. Stray lock of pale hair escaping over her forehead.

An inebriated man brushed against me. "Sorry." His Australian accent entered my field of awareness. I barely noticed him. I was too fixated on her.

The woman was in a prime photo spot, under a central arch whose filigreed support held the heaviest concentration of locks on the bridge. She rested, knees up, a blanket wrapped around her shoulders, a paper cup held out to the unspeaking, unseeing tourists walking by.

How could they miss her? She had stationed herself on purpose, at the crest of the bridge, under the bouquet of locks that clung to the peeling white paint of the iron.

There was a sense in my belly and my chest. A feeling. A knowing tension stopped me in my tracks.

This was the time. I had to leave an offering. Right here.

This beggar could not be ignored.

She was a special one, the only bit of living magic on this hope-for-magic bridge. A messenger. A harbinger. A sign. The Street Gods needed to be acknowledged, and she was their unknowing go-between.

That was how my magic worked. I had to feel the rightness of it inside my solar plexus. Feel the tugging of the threads that said it was the correct place. And the proper day and time. The right phase of the moon on river water.

The wind whipped around me, but I didn't care anymore. There was work to do.

She didn't look like anything special. Could have been anyone. Perhaps the beggars shift their spots, trading choice corners or stoops in shifts. This street has more money, and that one tends toward softer hearts. But it didn't matter to me, not in that moment. In that moment, it was clear: she was stationed under those locks for me.

I paused, dug a coin purse from my leather bag, re-snapped the bracers against pickpockets, and walked toward her. Her pale, narrow face turned up, framed by dusk, paper cup incandescent white in the gloaming.

Her cup was empty. How could it be empty?

Her cup was waiting. Open.

My coins rattled in. As much as I had in the little leather coin purse. Likely five euro total. She thanked me softly. I couldn't place the accent, it was carried away by the noise of people and the wind.

And then I *saw* her.

It was as if the coins had activated her essence, causing speech and movement and an aliveness that wasn't there before, like an old carnival fortune teller behind glass, who spit out a fortune if you slid coins into the proper slot.

In the corners of my eyes, she appeared as something *other*. A faint. A haunt. A spirit. Fae. I couldn't get a read on her. My vision doubled in and out of focus. The continuous slow tide of people across the bridge was beginning to annoy me. I needed clarity. To see what and who she was.

If only I had some magical tools on me. Yeat's blade. The hazel wand I'd carved off one full moon, pouring cider at the roots of the tree. Or a black scrying mirror. Something.

A handful of coins and a cigarette. Those were what I had.

Likely a real magician could have done something with these tools, but I was a novice at actual magic. The Theoretician, that was me, despite my midnight fumbling.

Ever hopeful, yes, but I never expected that magic would wake up in front of me like this. Not on a bridge in the middle of Dublin, on my evening constitutional, when what I was really doing was avoiding another pint of beer.

This shit was too much.

But it was here. *She* was here.

The evening everything changed.

"What do you want?" Her voice should have been the raspy, hard used voice of a street sleeper and chronic cougher from too much damp night air. But it wasn't. Her voice was sweet. Sweet like water from a deep flowing well. The kind that rested under trees tied with healing wishes.

But I didn't need healing.

"I don't want anything. I just gave you some money." I shuffled back from her a bit. Back from her ice-blue eyes.

"You left an offering."

"What's the difference?"

She looked at me with scorn, mouth pursing up beneath her acorn of a nose. With a grumbling sound in her throat, she turned her face away from me, tugging the knit cap further down on her brow.

When she did that, the glimmering around her started to fade. The weird double vision was righting itself into just-an-ordinary-night again. The wind whispered that a pint was waiting for me, scant blocks away.

"Wait! Just…" crouching down, my knees almost touching her blanket, I willed her to look at me again. "Please. I just need a minute. Can you give me a minute?"

Blue eyes turned toward me again. She gestured at the bridge beside her. "Sit." The air wavered again, as if a low, sonic boom had gone off in the back of my skull.

Knees a little wobbly by that time, I sat. Hard.

The bridge was cold under my ass. My fingers twitched to light another cigarette, but I didn't want to break the moment. Or offend her. You never knew with people. Or with people who weren't people.

I turned toward her, but she was staring straight ahead, cup nowhere to be seen. I stared ahead, too. The lights and bridge railings, all the locks, they winked in and out between the bodies walking by. The night noises had become muffled. It was as if no one saw us. We were in some bubble outside space and time.

"What do you want?" she asked again.

Shit. I didn't know how to answer. Didn't know if it was safe to answer. Didn't know what the right answer was.

Didn't know.

But I did know I didn't want her to go away again. Not yet.

Taking a shaky breath of river scented air, I decided to risk it. Risk the thing I always push aside from my thoughts, or drowned in a pint of beer.

"I want magic."

"Seems to me you already have it," she mused. "If you didn't, you wouldn't have seen me, or even if you did, the offering couldn't have come through."

I chewed on that for a moment.

"I'm talking about *real* magic. Like, the ability to do things. To change things. The ability to..."

Her slight body shifted under the blanket. I wished I had a blanket. My ass was really getting cold, as were the tips of my fingers. I jammed my hands into my pockets. At least the wind had died down.

I could feel her staring at me, but didn't dare to look.

"You want the ability to what? Hear the language of the birds? Pick the plants that hex or heal? Write words that make people turn their lives inside out? Draw a lover to you? Make yourself rich?"

None of that. I shook my head. None of that was what I wanted. Well, not 100%. I wanted a lover. And some extra euros would be welcome, sure they would.

But what I really wanted? "I just want to know that it's all *real*."

She touched me. Right between my eyes.

High-pitched whining split my skull open, and everything flashed greenish light, then dark, then light again. I couldn't see, I couldn't hear except the skull splitting screeching. The taste of silver flooded my mouth. How did I know what silver tasted like? Then kumquats. Apricot jam. Black tea. Green plant shoots.

All the weirdness of the world shook through my body, and I knew. There was magic in the molecules that drifted off my skin and spun away into the sky. There was something. Something. Something. Some...

I came to, throat hoarse like I'd been screaming, collapsed over my knees, bridge vibrating with the people shoving themselves around me. My pants were wet and warm. I'd pissed myself. Shit. Shit. Shit. Shit.

My head was on her thigh. A soft hand stroked my hair.

"Open your eyes."

"It hurts." My head was fucking pounding.

"Shh. Open your eyes."

I did, and almost pissed myself again.

Strange small, furry beasts perched on people's shoulders, whispering in their ears. Stranger beings flew through the dusky air, throwing orbs of light at the crows, who shied away, rrracking. The flying beings were laughing, sounding like... I wasn't sure. Bells wasn't right. But neither was anything else I could think of.

I could hear things splashing in the river. A strange singing rose from under the bridge. So did a big rumbling noise, like boulders falling down a hill.

The night tasted different. More fresh. More alive somehow. Like the building stones were alive. The lamps. The river. The metal of the bridge.

The bridge. The locks were creaking and whispering above our heads.

"Lost in love. Locked in love. Are you happy yet?

Are you content? Do you love each other? Did you? Do you? Did you?"

The hairs stood up on my neck and a shudder racked my ribs.

"What is all this?" I croaked.

Her hand stopped stroking my head. "Magic. The in between. The seldom seen. The place you always sense but never quite taste or hear. You have the gift now, to be aware of it all."

She started stroking my hair again. "Do you still want it?"

I couldn't answer.

Then she shoved a bit at my shoulders, bony fingers clutching the meat of my bicep, encouraging me to sit up again. I groaned as I pushed my hands against the cold bridge, pulling myself into a sitting position, I almost blacked out again, as the pounding in my head increased.

"Holy...!"

"Just breathe slowly, you'll acclimate." She was holding out a silver flask. "Drink."

I took it. It should have been cool, but felt warm under my fingers. Strange glyphs were carved into the silver, limned in greenish light. No way did I want to drink what was in that flask.

But it intrigued me to be sure. No doubts about that.

"If I drink this, what'll happen to me?"

She laughed at that, like water gurgling over hard stones. "It should help ease the pounding in your skull. Help set you back to rights."

I unscrewed the little cap, prepared for a shock. The scent was apricots and pears. Tilting the flask against my lips, there was that warmth again, and then the liquid, warmer still. Some sort of brandy. Delicious. As soon as I swallowed, my head was soothed. Just like...

"Magic," she said.

"Yeah. Magic. What else can I expect from this?"

"Well, look up." I looked out across the river, up to the sky, which was now full dark.

"Not there," she said. "Up above your shoulders."

Craning my neck back, I saw a small, furred beastie, a little like a cat. Or a gargoyle. Or something like. It's fur was grey, with a white blaze at its neck, and black eyeliner around its green cat eyes.

"Allo," it rumbled at me. "Bout time yeh woke up, yeh daft bastard. Been waitin' long enough for yeh."

The woman beside me laughed her river laugh. "I don't think she was ready for the likes of you, Mogwallach."

Mogwallach. I struggled to my feet, wet pants slapping against my thighs. Shit. I looked at the woman, then back at the beast.

"What is it?"

She smirked. "Why don't you ask him?"

Him. It was a him. "Mogwallach, what are you?"

He preened on the railing of the bridge. "I am a pooka-beast that seems to have nought better to do w me time than to mess w the likes of yeh."

"I thought pookas were all horses."

Mogwallach snorted through his little cat nose. "Thas what yeh get fer readen daft books all the day long. Yeh got to *taste* the magic teh know the magic."

It was all I could do to not reach out and touch his fur. To see if he was real. But I had the sense that would offend him, so I shoved my hands back into my pockets and concentrated on ignoring my clammy jeans.

"Give us an arm, will yeh?"

Taking a deep breath, I held out my right arm toward him, and Mogwallach clambered up onto my shoulder. I was glad to be wearing wool thick enough to not feel whatever claws were on his six toed feet. A weight settled on my shoulder.

I looked around. Then it hit me. The people with the beasts... "Do all these other people work magic?"

The woman spoke. "If only they did. We do the best we can, here in the in-between. Talking to the one's with some potential. We whisper in music. We trip people who need to pause a moment. We tug on a shirt sleeve and tell people to look. Sometimes it works. Sometimes it doesn't. Sometimes we just give up...

And not all of us are kind," she finished.

That made me shiver again.

"Let's be gettin' on, mate, before yer pants start to stink."

"Good idea." The scents and sights of the ordinary world rushed back in, companion to the magic world I now couldn't figure out how I had missed. I wanted a beer now. And my stomach rumbled for dinner, suddenly hungry. But Mogwallach was right. I needed to change into clean pants.

But. "Hey," I said.

She looked up at me. Waiting.

"Thank you. You can't know how much this means to me…"

The woman waved a hand, as if to say, "'Tis nothing."

But it was. It was a lot.

"Will you be here again? Can I come talk to you?"

Her blue eyes were steady on mine. "I'm around."

The locks were still whispering their strangeness. "Barbed hearts. Locked hearts. Souls without keys. Did you? Do you? Love her?"

I was glad I'd never hooked my heart to anyone else's here.

She and I glanced at one another for just one moment, before I walked away, pooka on my shoulder, toward lights and noise and a clean set of jeans, and dinner with a pint of Smithwicks.

There are compacts that need to be held, and promises met, on bridges in strange cities.

She could have been anyone. But this night, she was there for me.

Then I realized: I never caught her name.

4

THE STARS OF NEVERWHERE

ho would save Samuel Lee?
That was where he was in the current story.

Things had grown so strange, he honestly didn't know if he could take it anymore. The stack of library books piled on the floor wasn't helping. Neither was his favorite playlist.

All he could do was return to the story inside his head. The one he'd been making up since he was seven and a half and the strange man had moved in next door. Samuel was ten now.

The man seriously creeped Samuel out. Samuel started crossing the street rather than cross in front of the cottage next door, certain the man would leap out and snatch him away one day.

"Just don't pay attention to him, Samuel," his mother said. "He's just a sad, angry man, and it has nothing to do with you."

She didn't know. The library books taught Samuel that parents were often oblivious to what was truly going on. Adults tended to see what was on the surface and missed the sideways places.

The sideways places were the most important things, Samuel knew.

They glimmered and beckoned and called. Things entered and did not return. Other things emerged.

Like the man.

The rain fell in steady, drenching sheets, the way it had been for twenty-five days, non-stop. It grew a little lighter at times and whipped up wind and trees in the middle of the night, but mostly, it was the same, straight down, a monochrome fall of wet.

Samuel didn't mind, except it made it harder to keep his books dry. And it obscured his view of the sideways places. He figured he should feel relieved by that, but he knew that not being able to see or hear whatever was there was worse than seeing and hearing. He could still *feel* something. He just had no idea what was there.

The man next door really had stepped out of the sideways places one day. That was the thing his mother didn't understand.

"Oh, he just moved his things in when we were gone that Saturday. Don't you remember? We went to see Spiderman, and out for ice cream after."

But Samuel had seen him. He had seen him slide through the shimmering air in his hunched black coat and slope-crowned, broad-brimmed black hat, with his skin as white as moonlight on birch bark, and his chin and cheekbones sharp as knives. The man didn't have much nose to speak of, and it was hard to see his eyes.

Samuel felt the man stare at him that day. It was the last sunny day before the rains hunkered down in earnest that year. The last day of Autumn before the Winter came.

The man paused, the top of his face shaded into darkness by the hat, the white lower half of his face gleaming, and looked –Samuel was sure of it!– straight into Samuel's eyes. Then the man scuttled around the back side of the house next door.

There was no moving truck. No car full of boxes. Just a man who stepped out from a narrow slit in the shadows into the sun.

Things were okay for the first year or so. The man scuttled out now and then, but mostly stayed in the hulking cottage that used to be cute, with neat little curtains and a tidy stoop. But month after month, the house took on a more gloomy cast, even at the height of summer.

Then the rains returned.

And the neighborhood cats began to disappear.

At first, no one noticed. They figured the cats were hunkering down under houses or deep in the bushes somewhere, waiting for a break in the downpour.

The break in the rain never came. And neither did the cats. They insisted on going out, morning, noon, or night. And they simply failed to return.

Their humans stood, holding offerings of tuna and kibble, on broad porches and back stoops, and called the cat's use-names off the balconies of the apartment complex on the corner. The shouted names and rattling of food boxes disappeared beneath the steady sound of falling water.

And Samuel Lee? Samuel played cards with his Oma, did his homework, played online video games with his best friend Hal, and went to school. He tried to not pay attention to the rapidly crumbling cottage next-door, to the winds that whipped the tree branches and rattled his windowpanes every night. He tried to ignore the steady drenching rain.

But most of all, Samuel tried to pay no attention to the man next door.

Oh, he still saw him. Samuel saw the man all the time now. Out of the corner of his eyes, the man was waiting. When Samuel stepped off the school bus in the afternoons, he saw the shadow of the man's hat and the rain that bounced off the brim. But when he turned to look, all he would see was a mailbox, or a tree stump, or sometimes nothing at all.

Who would save Samuel Lee? The story was at a standstill. All he knew was that he was in danger.

S piny hands grabbed at his arms. Spiny fingers turned his face. The fingers were like claws, like knives. Samuel lashed out with elbows and the heels of his winter boots. He struggled against his raincoat, tried to slip his arms out of the backpack that felt like it weighed 1000 pounds. Rainwater sluiced down his face, into his ears, his mouth, even up his nose. Samuel gasped and sputtered and fought and flailed.

"Get off me!" Samuel couldn't see what had attached itself to him, but if he had to place any bets, he would bet it was the man. "Let me go!" Samuel kicked out again, this time connecting with a shin. The spiny hands didn't lose their grip, not for one second. Samuel's mind raced, trying to remember what he learned from the three months of kid's judo his mother had forced him to take the year before.

He went limp, and all the fight dropped from his body at once. Startled, the hands let go.

Samuel ran.

He ran all the way toward the tan brick bulk of the library, where he was supposed to meet Hal and work on their history assignment. Dragging open the heavy wooden glass doors he flung himself into the shadowed vestibule, and stood panting, dripping water on the gray mat covering the marble floor. He peered through one of the panes of glass, but all he could see were the bare maple branches, waving in the wind, some cars, and the steady rain.

Samuel swept the hood off his head, wiped his face, and entered the library.

The library had been one of his favorite places since he was small. He loved the smell of books, the quiet murmuring of the librarians, and the possibility that he just might find the answers he was looking for. He might even find out the answer to the question who would save Samuel Lee. But he was starting to doubt that. Especially now.

The rows of metal shelving filled with plastic wrapped spines of hardbacks made way to paperbacks, and finally, to the wooden study carrels. He could see the top of Hal's spiky blond hair already bent over some books. Hal was as much of a nerd as Samuel was.

Samuel quickened his pace until he was standing right next to Hal. He slung his backpack off, and dropped it like a weight to the floor. Then he shook himself out of his raincoat and draped it over the back of a wooden chair.

"Dude, you're soaked." Hal was always one to state the obvious. "You okay?"

Samuel dropped into his chair and leaned in close, lowering his voice, "I think that man tried to grab me."

"For real? The weird guy? What makes you think it was him? What happened?"

Samuel explained as best he could, but it sounded strange even to his ears. Hal looked interested, because nothing weird ever happened to him, but Samuel could tell he was skeptical. Skeptical. That was their word of the week.

"Maybe it was nothing. I don't know. But something grabbed me, that's for sure."

"Should we tell somebody?" Howell said. "Like the librarian? Maybe other kids are in danger."

Samuel thought about it for a moment, then shook his head. Who was there to tell?

He woke in the darkness. For once, the wind didn't lash the windows, and the rain had receded to a steady patter.

The man was in his room. Samuel could feel him. There was a disturbance in the air, the kind that let you know you weren't alone. And if he tried, he could hear someone breathing under the sound of the rain. Samuel lay very still. He tried to think of what to do. Should he yell? Call his parents?

That didn't seem right. Samuel didn't know how he knew it, he just did. The man was mysterious, and maybe he made the cats disappear, but Samuel hadn't heard any stories of children disappearing.

He made his decision. Quick as lightning, he reached out for his Buzz Aldrin lamp and flicked it on.

The man peered out from underneath his broad-brimmed hat, his eyes still in shadow, his cheekbones like knives.

"What do you want?" Samuel whispered.

The man cleared his throat. It sounded like rocks tumbling down the hills onto the highway. It was strange. Samuel realized he didn't feel afraid anymore. The old man wasn't exactly a friendly neighbor, and maybe he was still some freak from the sideways worlds, but he was also just someone who happened to be sitting in Samuel's bedroom in the middle of the night.

Yeah... Maybe it was a little weird. Maybe Samuel was a little bit weird.

"She thinks you're ready." The man's voice carried all the weight of winter. It was filled with long, dark nights, the feeling of ice on the back of your neck, and the taste of rain.

"Who? Who thinks I'm ready?"

The man shook his head, just slightly, enough to shake the edges of the brim of that dark hat.

"If you're willing, put on your shoes and come with me." The man stood, coat pooling around his ankles, white fingers emerging from the cuffs, face still half-shadowed.

Guess it's up to you now, Samuel Lee, Samuel thought. He flipped back his Crab Nebula comforter and swung his feet to the cold floor.

S amuel carried his shoes down the stairs, pausing in the kitchen to slip them on and lace them. His coat hung on a hook near the back door. The air in the kitchen was cold and smelled like spaghetti sauce. He was glad he'd pulled a sweatshirt on over his pajamas. Buttoning the coat up all the way, he stepped outside. It was dark. But the rain was letting up, which was good. Samuel didn't feel like getting soaked again. He'd had enough of that lately. Everyone complained about the rain, and not just the usual complaints, because it rained every winter. But not like this, the people said. Not like the last three years.

Not like since the man moved in.

"This way," the man said. Samuel followed him into the dark of the garden towards the back gate. The gate swung open quietly on its well-oiled hinges. Something skittered through the bushes. Opossum, Samuel figured. A yellow streetlamp marked the space between Samuel's parents' home and the man's cottage. The man slid around the pool of light, and it set the edges of his hat and coat gleaming. Samuel wondered why he didn't walk straight through, but he figured better follow whatever it was the man was doing.

That was what the stories always told you. When someone came from a place that wasn't earth, you either ran as fast as you could, or you did exactly what they did. Because you never knew what misstep might end up trapping you.

You never knew what thing you ate or drank or said meant that you'd never see your family and home again.

They walked behind the cottage, and Samuel stifled a gasp. While the cottage was falling down, the garden had flourished.

Secret hollows were covered in ivy. Japanese Maples brooded over stones. From a back corner, Samuel caught the slight trickling sound of a water-fall. And, in the center of it all, circling row after row of blooming roses.

Samuel moved toward them, sniffing their perfume. Then he saw that the bushes weren't quite right. Some of the bushes were in full bloom, others were tipped with delicate buds, and interspersed between them all were the bare rosebushes of winter, fat rosehips gleaming red in the mottled light and dark.

"What is this place?"

There was no answer, so Samuel just followed the man, who seemed to be leading him directly towards the center of the rosebush circles. Samuel understood now why the cottage was so neglected; all the man's attention must've gone back here.

There was an opening between one bush filled with deep red roses, and another of the winter bushes whose rose hips were bigger than any Samuel had ever seen.

His Oma put rosehips into honey and ate them all winter long. Samuel liked the combination of tart and sweet. Mama said it was the best way to get vitamin C.

Oma was never sick, so they both must be right.

"Where are you taking me?"

The man just flicked his spiny knife fingers forward. Samuel followed.

And there she was. He could swear she hadn't been there seconds before, but she was there now.

Surrounded by roses, hair pale as moonlight

tumbled down her shoulders until it almost reached the ground. The ground that was covered with maple leaves, oak leaves, ginkgo leaves, and the petals of pink and yellow roses. The man bowed deeply, sweeping the broad-brimmed hat off his head for just a moment. Samuel could see he was bald. And then the man stood tall again, hat back on his head, face in shadow. Leaving Samuel to stand and stare.

Her face was all flat planes and hollows, her skin the color of the walnut dresser in his Oma's room. Three birch trees shook their silvery leaves, their bark as pale as her hair. Like the old man's skin.

"Who are you?" Samuel asked the question, but he knew. He knew exactly who she was. And the man? He must be some sort of messenger or something. Kings and queens always had messengers, didn't they?

She spoke. Her voice sounded the way Samuel imagined a glacier cracking would sound.

"I am the Queen of Winter," she said. "And I have been waiting for you."

It didn't explain the cats. Later that night, back in bed, that was the thought that flickered through Samuel's mind.

What happened to the cats?

The hems of his pajamas were damp around his feet. He shivered beneath the Crab Nebula comforter and burrowed more deeply into his flannel pillow. Out of all the things he wondered, maybe that was a little strange, but Samuel wanted to know. He had a hard time falling asleep that night, but he finally did.

She should have been terrifying, but she wasn't. Instead, Samuel found himself wishing that instead of a rose garden at night they were sitting in front of the fireplace in his favorite rocking chair, the one so big he could sit cross-legged in it, a book propped on his lap. He would offer her the special hot chocolate his father made, the one with spices in it. She would like it, he was sure.

Instead, he stood shivering in the winter garden staring at the flat planes of her face, wondering why she called him there.

"I need the ones who see what isn't there," she said. "We always watch for the ones who pay attention. You've been seeing us for years, haven't you?"

Samuel froze in place, pinned like a beetle on a board. She was right. When he was five, he tried to tell his mother about it. She'd ruffled his hair and complemented his imagination. "But I'm not..." She smiled and told him to draw a picture.

So he did. He had notebooks filled with pictures that he would share only with Hal. Together, they made up stories about the sideways worlds and the people who lived there.

But he never thought to see one like this. Standing directly in front of him, with a voice like a glacier, and hair like the moon.

"I was never sure it was real," he said. "I mean, I only ever caught glimpses, you know?"

She nodded gravely. "That was by design."

Samuel shuffled his feet a little. His toes were getting cold. He cleared his throat. "So, um, the man, he said..."

"That I was waiting for you."

"Yeah."

"Follow me."

Samuel didn't remember what happened after that. All he knew was that the man was carrying him up the stairs to his bedroom. The spiny white fingers helped him off with his boots and tucked him into bed, leaving Samuel awake with his thoughts.

N ight after night it happened. The man would wake him up, or sometimes Samuel would be reading, and the man would come. Samuel had learned to dress more warmly for bed. Sometimes it was raining now, sometimes not. And then the snow came.

The garden was white with it. Hushed with it.

Except for the ring of roses. The ring of roses looked as it had before. And there she was, with her moonlight hair and her walnut face arms crossed over her velvet chest.

"Are you ready this time?"

Samuel knew exactly what she was talking about. He nodded. "I want to go," he said.

And that was the truth; he *did* want to go. It had just taken him a while to work up to it. He finally figured out what had happened that first night. He had fainted. That was embarrassing, but oh well. The only thing that bugged him now about the situation was the fact that he hadn't told Hal. He just couldn't quite figure out how to talk to his best friend about it. Out of all the freaky stuff they discussed, this was a little too freaky.

But Hal would be pissed off that he hadn't invited him along. Maybe next time. After reconnaissance.

After Samuel had figured out exactly where this was leading.

He didn't see the doorway, the gateway, the what-ever-it-was. One minute they were in the middle of the roses with snow sprinkling the garden all around them, and the next thing they were in a brick hallway —a corridor, the fantasy books called it. Torchlight sputtered and flared, lighting up the stones. Like, *real* torchlight. Iron rings bolted into the walls with flaming sticks thrust into them.

"Cool," Samuel whispered. He followed the long trailing velvet skirts of the Winter Queen. He could feel the man in the broad-brimmed hat behind. Samuel didn't know if that should make him feel safe or afraid. He shrugged. Might as well just go with it.

The hallway opened onto a vast hall with tall, vaulted ceilings held up by carved wood beams. There was an itching at the back of Samuel's eyes. He started to tear up. Then he sneezed.

Looking down at the flagstone floor he finally figured out where the cats had gone. There they were, dozens and dozens of them. Big orange bruis-ers, mottled tabbies, Siamese, even a Persian or two. They lapped at dishes of cream, reclined on fluffy cushions, or played with endless balls of red and yellow yarn.

Samuel laughed and laughed and laughed. The room was so huge his voice felt swallowed up. When he looked at the woman, she had a smile on her face.

"And that is why we called you here today. Our

hob is sick. We need someone to care for all these cats."

"I don't get it," Hal said. "Why would the Queen of Winter need you to take care of the neighborhood cats? And why'd the cats run away in the first place?"

The boys were in Samuel's room, supposedly working on a science-art project. Popsicle sticks, glue, and construction paper littered the floor. The room smelled like the hot chocolate Samuel's dad had delivered half an hour ago. Samuel peered into his white mug. Yep. All gone.

"I'm not really sure. Not yet. None of it makes sense to me, though Strickleton says it 'will all be clear in time.' As if."

"Strickleton's the creepy guy next door? Why doesn't *he* take care of the cats?"

"I asked him that," Samuel replied.

Strickleton sniffed, a sniff that seemed too mighty to come from his tiny nose. His rocks-rolling-down-the-hill voice rumbled, "I," he said, "am the Gardener."

Just like that. Capital letter and everything. Gardeners, it turned out, did not take care of cats. Everyone in Sideways had a job and wasn't allowed to do anyone else's. And yeah, the hob who held the title of Cat-Herder was sick.

"You are perfect," the Winter Queen said. "We always offer gifts to the observant children like yourself. You shall grow up blessed, touched by our realms."

She'd paused then, and tilted her head his way. "Do you have a longing to be a poet?" she asked. "A bard? A painter, perhaps?"

"I want to be an astronomer!" Samuel blurted out.

The Winter Queen looked a bit disappointed at that. "Ah. I see. Well, the stars are nice, I suppose. We have different constellations here," she said. "We shall show them to you next time you come." The queen paused then, to drink deeply from a pretty golden cup. "If, that is, you agree to care for the cats for four phases of the moon."

Samuel rubbed at his eyes. He would really like to see the Sideways constellations. But there was the one problem...

"I'm allergic."

"So you have to help me!" he said to Hal. "You love cats, right? And didn't Moggie run away last year? I bet she's there! You could find her again. Bring her home!"

Hal didn't look too keen about the prospect.

"I don't know Samuel, you sound kind of crazy, you know?" Hal was gluing popsicle sticks together, trying to form a geodesic dome. "We're not little kids anymore."

Samuel paced the carpet in his small bedroom, from bed to desk, to the door. He skirted around Hal, waving his arms with excitement.

"Don't you see? All those books we've read, all the stories..." Samuel stopped and flopped back down on the floor. He leaned toward his friend, whose blonde hair was even more spiky than usual. Samuel wondered if Hal had accidentally-on-purpose rubbed some glue into his hair. "What if they're true?"

Hal sat down two triangles on a piece of news-paper to dry. "I don't know, Samuel. I have enough trouble getting my parents to let me come over to your house. You really think they're going to let me traipse off to wherever it is?"

"But that's the beauty of it," Samuel said. "They won't know."

S ure enough, Samuel convinced Hal to join him. Samuel figured if he brought someone to take care of the cats—though he still wasn't sure why exactly the cats had gone to the sideways world—then maybe, just maybe, as a reward, the Queen of Winter would let them both see the stars.

"Holy shit," Hal said.

"I know, right?" Samuel looked around the hall, still impressed by the vaulted ceiling, the crisscross of wooden beams, and all the cats.

He turned to the man in the slouch-brimmed hat. "Do we wait here?"

The man started to walk, threading a pathway through the cats. His bone white lifelike fingers gestured them forward. Hal looked at Samuel. Samuel just shrugged and loped after the man's dark coat.

Hal tugged at Samuel's coat sleeve. "This is like some Dungeons & Dragons stuff," he whispered. Samuel nodded again and kept moving. He just hoped this deal was going to work.

They entered a brick hallway lit with the same sconces, flames casting red and gold shadows everywhere. It was strangely medieval. Samuel wondered if all the sideways worlds were like this, or if it was just this one in particular. Maybe the Queen of

Winter just liked it this way. He wondered if the torches were magical, or if there was a Torch-Lighting-Hob that took care of them.

Just as suddenly as the corridor began, it ended, this time opening into a smaller room. The ceilings were just as high, but the walls were close in, forming a cozy space. Fire crackled in an enormous hearth which was flanked by two wolfhounds who twitched their ears and slit opened their eyes. Checking for danger? The dog on the left sighed and closed its eyes again. The dog on the right stretched and yawned, then trotted over to a large comfortable chair where the Queen of Winter sat, reading a book. Samuel would've expected a big tome with gilded edges, but it looked like an ordinary paper book from home. In her other hand, she held a half-eaten apple. The dog sat at her feet and whined. She looked up.

"Ah," she said, "I see you brought a friend to meet me." She held up the book. It looked familiar. "Do you like A Wrinkle in Time?"

It was one of Samuel's favorite books. "I love it."

The dark planes of the Winter Queen's face arranged themselves into what Samuel supposed was a smile. "Then I'm sure will be great friends."

She turned her eyes on Hal, who stood frozen to the spot.

"Are you the new Cat-Herder? You don't look like a hob. You look like a boy," she said.

Hal blushed, all the way from his T-shirt to his spiky blond hair. "Uhhh... Yes, ma'am. I'm just..."

The Queen tilted her head in question. Then she clapped her hands, "I know! You are a Bard! I can see it all around you. You must also be a friend of the Wind."

Samuel's jaw dropped. He stared at his friend, who only grew redder in the face. Hal sketched a shallow bow, then straightened up again.

"At your service, my Queen."

Wow. This sure was getting interesting, Samuel thought.

"How delightful," the Winter Queen said. "An Astronomer and a Bard." She turned to the man in the hat. "Well done, Strickleton. But what are we to do with all these cats?"

Strickleton moved forward, just as Hal burst out, "I'll take care of them!" Strickleton stopped in his tracks.

"Well, well, well," the Winter Queen said, "a Bard and a Cat-Herder combined. This is turning out better than I ever imagined. Would anyone care for some tea?"

A nd so the adventure began. Every evening between homework and bed, for four cycles of the moon, Hal would whistle at Samuel's window and off the boys would sneak to the hollow of roses in Strickleton's garden. Samuel studied of the constellations in the sideways realm while Hal brushed five cats a night in turn. The cat-herding hob did not return, so the boys continued.

After six months or six days or six years of this, the Queen of Winter rewarded Samuel with the most clever and cunning telescope and astrolabe he'd ever seen. For Hal, she procured a lute.

The cats, it turned out, liked the cream from the Sideways world better than the cream at home. Plus, there was always a soft cushion or a warm hearth to be had.

Mostly? The cats hated the rain.

A nd so the boys grew up together, making music and gazing at stars. Years later Hal became both a rock musician and a poet of some renown. He raised Maine Coon Cats in his spare time when he wasn't recording or on tour.

And Samuel Lee? It turned out he didn't need saving at all. He fell in love nine times, helped to raise three children, and mapped areas of space no one even knew existed before.

He also wrote illustrated children's books. The title of his most beloved work was *The Stars of Neverwhere.*

It's still in print today.

5

THE ICE CREAM VAN

He stood in front of the open Sub Zero. Mustard. Some salad greens. An expired carton of rice milk. Cheese. Neatly contained and stacked leftovers of grilled fish, sauteed vegetables, rice.

The cold washed over his face and began creeping down the rest of him. He could smell an old, escaped onion in there somewhere. Somewhere in the back of the crisper, no doubt.

John shut the refrigerator door. The kitchen felt empty. All chrome and glass with a temperature-controlled wine room off the pantry. He shook his head slightly. Sank to the slate floor. She was never coming back.

Ba dum, ba dum, ba dadaddum, ba dum ba dum ba DUH dum!

The tinkling, slightly out of phase, sound of chimes came through the open window. Ice cream. Bad ice cream. Cheap ice cream. Ice cream sandwiched between two long, softening chocolate wafer cookies. Ice cream in a cone, covered in hard chocolate and nuts. Ice cream on a stick. Fudgesickles.

John was quickly on his sneaker'd feet, patting the pockets of his track suit for change. There was money on the entry table. He'd left it there three days ago, after Carol broke up with him at Le Lune and he'd crawled home and sobbed himself to sleep on their king-size bed with its 700 count navy sheets and pillow top mattress.

She had already rented a fucking condo across town. Would send movers for the things she wanted in a week or so. The condo was a different look, you know, so the things from the house wouldn't really fit, overall.

She had left the house that morning without mentioning a word.

"You must be joking!" He had shoved his glass of wine across the starched tablecloth, coming perilously close to knocking into the candles. Carol's manicured hand steadied the squat glass tumbler filled with glass beads and black tea light. Her fingernails were always these weird perfect ovals with white tips. They matched her sleek mahogany hair and her sharply tilted eyebrows.

"You've been considering this for what? A month? Three months? A year?"

She just sipped her Malbec and looked at him with those green eyes. Tinted contact lenses. "We've been drifting, John. You know that. You haven't been yourself in quite some time."

No. He hadn't been *her* in quite some time. He didn't match her nails and eyebrows and perfect hair. He had loved her. Still loved her. He'd tried and clearly failed.

John carefully pushed back his chair and rose.

Kissed her pale, powdery cheek. Then threaded through the other tables and out the door, leaving it to her to pay the check.

The chimes grew louder. The truck was almost in front of the house. He jogged toward the cherry wood console and the brass dish set under the Chinese vase with its now drooping bouquet. Under the keys and change he saw a five-dollar bill. He pocketed it all and ran out the door.

The ice-cream van was chugging up the little rise. Bright blue and yellow it rolled, incongruous, past the green sweeps of grass, the curving driveways, and the Tudor facades. How had it even gotten through the gate? Past the guard shack?

Then John noticed there were strange paintings on the side panels. Hedgehogs dancing. Otters drinking tea. A bear reading a gilded book. The van began to slow, stopping in front of the walkway at 836 Jasmine Drive. The jasmine actually still sweetened the air, despite attempts to tame the unruly vines by the homeowners' association. Fascists.

John stepped carefully toward the van, some of his excitement ebbing as the strange reality before him registered. The side window rolled up with a snap. Down plopped a hinged yellow counter. And behind the counter was the most amazing sight of all. A man? A man. Attenuated. Spindly. Spidery. Thin. With a tall top hat and a faded black frock coat. Out of his breast pocket peeked a red and white striped puff of silk. He didn't look like an ice cream vendor. He looked interested. And interesting.

"Come forward, my friend! I have treats in store! I have lavender ices and chocolate drops. I have licorice as black as a raven's mouth and ice cream as smooth as a selkie's thighs."

John's heart was beating funny, and he had a weird taste in his mouth. Like that one time Carol had made him try Chartreuse at that fancy French Quarter restaurant when he'd flown down to join her on some business trip. Strangely spicy and sugary at the same time. His eyes played tricks, too. It seemed like there were things creeping up on him, but when he turned his head, all he saw was concrete and tarmac, Tudor homes and green.

"I don't know what that means. I just wanted some ice cream. You got ice cream sandwiches? Vanilla?"

The man behind the counter looked disappointed. His sharp mouth turned down a bit. Then turned upward again.

"I think I know what you'll like! Rose petal ice cream delicately placed between cacao shortbread!" He bent, head obscured by the wall of the van. John stared at an otter. It stared back. He could hear rummaging and muttering. The man finally rose again, proffering—that was really the only word for it—a bar wrapped in bronze waxed paper.

Fumbling in his pocket, John pulled out the five.

The man waved his slender fingers in the air. "No, no! No payment required! This is our gift to you!" He placed the cool bar in John's hand, withdrew his arm, flipped up the counter and slammed down the window.

"Toodle-oo!" He called out from the front seat.

The van started rolling. The chimes began again, *Ba dum, ba dum, ba dadaddum, ba dum ba dum ba DUH dum!*

John shrugged, then peeled back a corner of the bronze paper. The cookie inside was thicker than the usual chocolate wafers. He sniffed at the bar. Sure enough: rose. The ice cream was pale colored, like vanilla, but with the smallest hint of pink. He peeled back more paper, ripping it as it went. Bit in. The cookie resisted for a moment, then the cold hit his teeth.

And a wash of butter, chocolate, fine ground wheat, and smooth, smooth cream tinged with rose fell through his mouth. John could barely chew. It was as if his body, as if time itself, had slowed. He almost stopped breathing. He licked at a droplet of the rosy cream before it fell onto his hand, then bit through the buttery chocolate and into the ice cream again. He closed his eyes and chewed. Swallowed.

Breathed in the scent of jasmine and sun touched grass.

"Selkie's thighs," he whispered. "Selkie's thighs."

They all hungered for something. Love. Acceptance. Recognition. Oh sure, sometimes they hungered for fame, or money, someone to control, or some eye candy that would prove their self worth, but all of those really boiled down to the first three.

Henri piloted the ice-cream van past tan and brown houses. Past white houses. Green lawns. Gardens with carefully tended roses, red and yellow. Gardens with low creeping phlox in blues and pinks. The occasional maple. It was *almost* beautiful and made him long for home. Home of the endless space between dawn and twilight. Home of the rushing waterfalls and deep green moss. The world here felt so *flat* sometimes. The food was like chewing on tree bark. The music? Like the chimes on this van. Tinny. Non-melodious. But they were comforting to them somehow, those chimes. To those who could hear them at all.

The ones who heard the chimes were filled with greater needs than most.

They were hungry for some magic.

The next day, John took a shower for the first time in days. He pulled on dark jeans and a t-shirt and padded barefoot to the closet. There, tucked in the back, was a long-sleeved purple shirt with a sharp-pointed collar that he'd bought four years ago and worn once.

He'd started out that evening feeling good. The purple set off his blue eyes in the mirror. Carol hadn't said a word, just paused and gave him the silent up and down.

The party was a disaster. Their friend Tim had sidled over with a beer, tilted it at John's shoulder, "Feeling happy today, John?" He started laughing. Smacked him on the back. "Hey Jerry, don't you think John's looking *happy*?"

Assholes. The shirt felt good as he pulled it on. Smooth cotton. Crisp. It tucked in flat and narrow around his body. He turned sideways and forward in the mirror, checking all the angles. Yeah. Purple.

That ice cream was fantastic. John definitely would keep his ears open for the chimes. Not that he'd be staying in this neighborhood for long. Funny, too, that he'd never seen the truck before, not in all the years they'd lived here. He'd never tasted anything like that ice cream sandwich either. Carol didn't allow ice cream in the house, but he sometimes hit the gelato shop when he was running errands in the city. The gelato was good, creamy, flavored with cardamom or raspberry. But nothing tasted like that rose. Or those cookies.

"Selkie's thighs. I wonder what the hell he meant by that."

John had woken with the memory of the ocean, salt spray on his lips, the feel of wind on his face. He'd been dreaming of the sand. Dreaming of the ways the white foam tickled the shore into soft dampness. Dreaming of the blue green of the waves. He'd heard singing. Some melody he couldn't place. A song he knew, but hadn't heard before.

He had awakened with tears on his face, but no real sadness. The feeling was more like...longing? Something he hadn't felt since he was a boy. He remembered reading books at night, curled under the coverlet, glow-in-the-dark stars winking from the ceiling. Sometimes he would put the book down, stare at those stars, and just be filled with so much *feeling*. He was never sure exactly what the feeling was, only that he *wanted* something. It wasn't that he wanted to get on a rocket ship to the stars. It wasn't that he wanted to fight a dragon, or quest for a missing goblet. He didn't want the freaky carnival to come to town, though that sounded pretty cool...

He just wanted *something*. He wanted something to *happen*. Nothing ever did.

For the first time, he felt like it just might. And if it didn't, perhaps he could do something about that.

Yeah, today just might end up being a good day.

The ice-cream van had seemed a lark. Henri had grown weary of the beauty all the time. The sameness and perfection. Here, he got to see different things. He got to travel down alleyways strewn with discarded needles, oil a gorgeous sheen upon the street. He had traveled into towns tucked high into dry mountains smelling of balsam and loam. Had driven past bodegas and delicatessens, pulled up in front of strip joints and movie theaters. He'd driven from ocean to ocean, to tattered board-walks and pristine sands. He'd given out kite shaped popsicles in East Oakland and white chocolate bonbons in Boulder. He'd driven through Detroit and Pittsburgh. Chattanooga and Crown Heights. Pulled up at a rodeo outside Bastrop and the symphony at Rockefeller Center.

Every single person he'd encountered man, woman, or child—prostitute or banker, football star or chemist, admin or mechanic—they'd all heard the chimes when no one else around them had. They all stepped forward to the yellow counter and asked for what they thought they wanted. It was never what

Henri had, but he always had just the thing. Not quite what they expected. Surprising. Delicate. Delicious.

Surprise. Yes. Sometimes he stayed just long enough to watch them shimmer with it as they sniffed and chewed and swallowed. Their faces would freeze for a moment. Then soften and relax. A shimmering light crept up into their eyes. He never stayed past that point, though. Never stayed long enough for them to ask him questions. That wasn't his job, answering things.

This world was either blinded, hurting, hungry, or numb. His job was to have just that little thing behind the counter. A taste of sweetness. A hint of darkness. The flavor of mystery, with the promise of some light.

With all of that, they could learn to feed the hunger on their own.

Once the magic was inside them... one less cardboard tasting dinner. One more tuneful song that caused loins to stir and hearts to wonder. One more book. One more painting. One more dance. One more building that called people to look and not pass by. One connection. Then another.

It would take some time. But Henri had that. And he had an ice-cream van.

READ AN EXCERPT OF THE NOVEL BY EARTH

I t was Solstice Eve, the longest night, and the coven had gathered. It was the time that ancient people thought the sun stood still in the sky before reversing itself.

Some said it was the night the sun would be reborn.

So much in her life was uncertain right now; Cassiel welcomed the moment of stillness and the promise of rebirth. Twenty-two years old and healthy, with a pretty enough face and a mass of curly red hair people admired...on the surface, Cassie's life looked pretty good.

Inside, though? She was worried all the time.

The slanted walls of Raquel's attic were painted creamy white, including to the knee walls. The dark planks of the fir floor gleamed in the light from the candles massed on altars in each corner of the space. Nine people sat on bright cushions in a rough circle.

Raquel was not only a coven mate, but Cassiel's boss at the café. A regal black woman with dread-locks flowing down her back, Raquel looked around the space, making certain everything was ready and in place.

A clap of her hands set a row of metal and beaded bracelets snapping on her wrists. Two more claps, and Cassiel felt her attention snap itself in place along the column of spine. She felt the rest of the coven exhale around her, and exhaled, too. Ready for magic. Ready for the night.

Raquel gestured toward the center of the room and Moss, a slender Japanese American man in his early twenties, picked up his athame, a double-bladed witch's knife, and began slowly turning in a circle. Cassie felt Moss's blade sweep by her, causing the edges of her skin to prickle and stand at attention.

She could almost see the blue flame she'd been told was the vital energy of magic, and of life itself. Prana. Mana. Essence. She certainly imagined it now, snaking from the blade tip as it traced the edge of the circle.

When he reached the place he had started from, the blade swept up in an arc overhead and then back down, forming a glowing sphere, a sphere of safety, a sphere to focus, a sphere of protection for those within and those without.

Cassie let her soul wander deeper. She let herself open to the magic of the night.

"Cassiel, is your cantrip ready?" Brenda said. The cantrip. The poetry that helped tune magical operations and rituals. Cassie was a poet, and the coven had started looking to her to weave spells of words.

Brenda had been Cassiel's main mentor for the year and a day of her coven apprenticeship. The white woman was in her early forties, with a messy array of brown hair piled on her head. As usual, she wore a flowing tunic over slim pants. Tonight's tunic was black, shot through with purple stars. A chunky silver pendant at her breast reflected the candlelight.

Cassie smoothed her hands on her jeans, tossed

the heavy fall of red curls over her shoulder and stood.

Stepping forward to face the north, she said "By earth…" She turned, pointing to each cross quarter in turn, charging up the energy, speaking as she went. "By flame. By wind. By sea. By moon, by sun, by dusk, by dark, by witches' mark…"

Cassie felt the energy build as the words moved through her. They were simple words, but like all magical poetry, their very simplicity increased the potency. What mattered was that they focused the witch's will. What mattered was that they called the planes of existence closer together, joining above and below, within and without.

"…We consecrate this holy ground, with sight, and sound, and breath twined 'round. With will and love, from below to above…"

Cassiel felt as if the whole hub of the cosmos spun around her, within her, and then locked into place. "Let the magic portals open," she said, then stood, vibrating in the hushed, still center of the space for one long breath. Then she bowed and took her place in the circle of the coven once again.

"So mote it be," eight voices responded.

Two other coveners, Alejandro and Lucy, carried a small table and a large black mirror into the center of the circle. The buttoned-up IT guy and the house painter, tall and short. Alejandro saw the future, and

Lucy did a lot of work with the ancestors. Those two couldn't have been more different, yet their magic fit together like dusk mirroring dawn.

"Tonight we scry," Raquel said. "We look into the other worlds to see what we can find there. We ask for guidance for the coming year. We ask for help. We ask for visions of what may be, and visions of that which must fall away, and we ask on this, the longest, darkest night, to feel the promise of new light. So mote it be."

Cassie was drifting in and out, between the worlds of matter and æther, feeling the weight of the longest night around her, feeling the magic in the room. She felt a sense of home, as she always did when surrounded by the Arrow and Crescent Coven. She could taste that sense of home, just like she could taste the mulled wine the coven had toasted with before heading up the stairs. The memory of it slept on the back of her tongue.

But she also had to admit the sense of home wasn't as strong as it was before, because even though she still let herself float in the in-between, her anxiety was back.

Cassie watched her coven mates move in and out in groups of two or three to kneel in front of the big black polished mirror, gazing into it, seeking prophecy or reassurance, a way forward or a way to release the past. She realized she was scared—terrified, actually, and growing more frightened by the minute.

The things that were in her past were things she had hoped to keep buried—the ghosts clamoring for her attention, day and night. The inquests. The police calling her for help on cases. Her fourteen-year-old self, shaking and stammering as she tried to testify on a witness stand, testify to things that no one should ever see. To things that no person except murderer and victim should ever know.

Except the victims were ghosts. And Cassiel could see them. Could hear their terrible stories, and see the images of their murders all too clearly in her head.

The ghosts were the reason she fled Tennessee.

"I can't do this," she whispered, "I can't, I can't do this."

Raquel moved towards her, put an arm around her shoulders. Her friend and boss drew Cassie in, and cradled her against her chest for a moment. Then, with a squeeze, she released her and turned Cassie's face toward her with her fingers.

"Cassiel," she murmured softly, "you are a child of the Goddesses and the Gods. You are beloved of this coven, and of the Goddess Diana herself, and we will not forsake you. Whatever it is you see tonight, I will personally help you bear it. You can do this. You got this, girl."

Cassie still felt the tension of sickness clamping down her throat and churning the mulled wine into a sour liquid in her belly as she nodded.

"Guess I'll get it over with," she said.

She moved forward with two other coven mates, Alejandro and her best friend in the coven, the elegant Selene.

She watched as they bowed their heads, gazing into the black expanse, Alejandro's face forming a sharply backlit profile. Selene's face was obscured by a fall of straight black hair. Then she leaned forward herself.

Staring into the black mirror was like staring into the curved bowl of space. Cassiel remembered nights out in the wilderness of Tennessee, coming upon a high place, nothing but black night and stars, so many stars, the kind you couldn't see in the city, the kind of stars she hadn't seen in years. Closing her eyes for a moment, she took three deep breaths and looked once again into the mirror. She saw the glimmering wink of candles, and the dark reflection of her own face. She saw a hand reaching out as though in friendship. She saw her parents. Her grandmother.

Feeling tension rising in her shoulders and belly again, she willed herself to calm down and drew in another deep breath.

"Help me see," she whispered to the mirror, "help me see what I need to see."

All of a sudden the mirror was wiped clean. There was nothing. Just blackness, deep, deep blackness. Cassie leaned in further, trying to keep her eyes soft as they wanted to focus, trying to find anything, something. "Show me, please." And there it was—an image of a burning tower. Cassie gasped and rocked back on her heels.

"No, no, no, no, no," she said.

She felt Raquel next to her. "You're fine, girl. Anoint yourself and look again." Raquel was holding out a small blue bowl of water.

"I don't think I can," Cassie replied.

Raquel was silent, still holding out the bowl. Cassie shook herself, dipped her fingertips into the bowl, then bathed her face and ran damp hands through the top of her hair. She lifted the heavy fall of hair and placed one cool, moist hand on the back of her neck and breathed.

It felt good. "Thank you," she whispered to Raquel, who nodded and moved back again.

Cassiel evened her breathing out and leaned toward the black mirror once again. Her eyes unfocused and Cassiel dropped into the black mirror. She was flying.

Flying through stars, flying through the air, then steering her spirit lower.

She was flying above the city of Portland and then she saw the room that her coven was in—she saw Alejandro and Selene, still kneeling by the black mirror, the other six lying down or sitting in a circle around the altar. She saw that some of them had left their bodies, shimmering silver cords attaching their spirits to their flesh.

She saw her own silvery cord and followed it down. It was as though her spirit were in two places at once, the observer and the observed. Cassie watched herself gazing in the mirror, and felt things go black again.

And then her eyes opened on to the face of a beautiful black woman with the strong, tall body of a warrior, a small tape recorder in one hand and a pen in the other.

"Who are you?" she asked.

"Who I am is not important. I don't exist here anymore, except as memories, ambitions, and work that still needs to be done. I need you to finish it because he can't. He's not able."

"Who? Who can't?"

The woman just shook her head.

"Follow the tower on fire."

"What? I don't understand. What do I need to do?" she asked.

The woman just looked at her with firm eyes, then scribbled something on a piece of paper.

"You will know," the woman said. *"Tell Joe I still love him. And tell Darius I said hi."*

The woman held up the piece of paper. Cassiel peered at it, trying to make out the word.

And then the woman was gone.

REVIEWS

Reviews can make or break a book's success.
If you enjoyed this book, please consider telling a friend,
or leaving a short review at your favorite booksellers or
on GoodReads.
Many thanks!

*Visit thorncoyle.com for a free short story collection
and to sign up for a monthly newsletter.*

ABOUT THE AUTHOR

T. Thorn Coyle has been arrested at least four times. Buy them a cup of tea or a good whisky and they'll tell you about it.

Author of the *The Witches of Portland*, the alt-history urban fantasy series *The Panther Chronicles*, the novel *Like Water*, and two story collections, her multiple non-fiction books include *Sigil Magic for Writers, Artists & Other Creatives*, and *Evolutionary Witchcraft*.

Thorn's work appears in many anthologies, magazines, and collections. They have taught magical practice in nine countries, on four continents, and in twenty-five states.

An interloper to the Pacific Northwest U.S., Thorn stalks city streets, writes in cafes, loves live music, and talks to crows, squirrels, and trees.

Connect with Thorn:
www.thorncoyle.com

With Steel to Hand

We Ride at Night

Single Novels and Story Collections

Like Water

Alighting on His Shoulders

Break Apart the Stone

Non-Fiction

Evolutionary Witchcraft

Kissing the Limitless

Make Magic of Your Life

Sigil Magic for Writers, Artists & Other Creatives

Crafting a Daily Practice

www.ingramcontent.com/pod-product-compliance
Lightning Source LLC
Chambersburg PA
CBHW060941120626
46557CB00003B/1098